High Seas

Doc's Study
At the Sunken Ship

Doc's
Lagoon

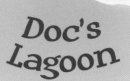

Island School

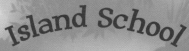

N

W   E

S

THE ADVENTURES OF

Blue Ocean Bob

A Challenging Job

B.O.B.®

Blue Ocean Bob

For Almira, Fred, and Jean—B.A.O.

For Hannah—K.S.K.

THE ADVENTURES OF
Blue Ocean Bob

A Challenging Job

by BROOKS OLBRYS

illustrated by KEVIN KEELE

Special thanks to Mary Morrissey for helping chart the course and
to Paola and Nicolas for setting the sails.

Design and composition by Greenleaf Book Group
Cover design by Greenleaf Book Group
Illustrations by Kevin Keele

ISBN: 978-0-9829613-5-3

16 17 18 19 20   10 9 8 7 6 5 4 3 2

First Edition

Library of Congress Control Number: 2014941637

Published by
Children's Success Unlimited LLC
250 Park Avenue, 7th Floor
New York, NY 10177

Printed in China
Manufactured by Oceanic Graphic International on acid-free paper
Manufactured in Guang Dong, China, September 2016
Batch No. TT16050967

Contents

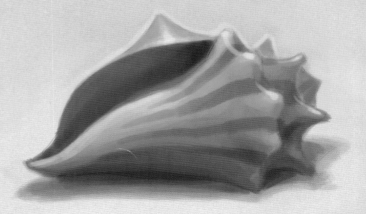

⇒ Chapter 1 ⇐
A Helping Hand

On the Island of Roses, there once lived a lad
who was looking for more than the things that he had.
He discovered his passion to safeguard the sea
and finally knew what he wanted to be.
He adopted the nickname of Blue Ocean Bob
and decided to master this challenging job.

But Xena, Bob's hummingbird guardian, feared
this job might be tougher than it first appeared.
"You've had a good start Bob, but I'm still concerned.
There are so many things that you haven't yet learned."
"I know," Bob admitted, "I set a big goal.
But something tells me I was meant for this role."

Bob had a mentor, Miss Mary Marine,

the finest sea expert his island had seen.

But she didn't mince words: "We've a promise to keep.

We must help a young seal learn to swim in the deep."

"The deep?" answered Bob. "I've been there in my boat.
And once on a dolphin—it's pretty remote!"

"Good training," said Mary. "But now you'll jump in.
To help Kodi learn, you must join her and swim.
If you think that you need some more time to prepare,
I suggest you see Doc at his rock over there."

Doc was a turtle and Mary's close friend.
On Doc's trusted wisdom, young Bob could depend.

So Bob left the pier. Xena just rolled her eyes.
For her it was cloudy, but Bob saw blue skies.
They arrived at the rock, but old Doc wasn't there.
He was down in his study, asleep in his chair.
Bob knocked on the ship, and Doc finally rose,
pushing his spectacles back on his nose.

"Hey, Doc! Are you down there? I hope you're awake.

A seal needs some training; her mom needs a break.

I'm not sure I can help since I don't scuba dive.

But I know there are skills she must learn to survive."

Doc swam out of his ship and stood up next to Bob.

He knew he could help with this difficult job.

"To teach well," Doc advised, "you must first learn a lot.

For how can you give what you haven't yet got?

You are a fine swimmer, Bob. That you have shown.

You just need some time in the sea on your own.

So go snorkel out and don't rush back too soon.

For the training you need, you must leave this lagoon.

And when you return, you can do so with pride.

You'll have learned that true confidence comes from inside."

"All right," answered Bob. "I will do as you say.
But Xena, please join me and help scout the way."

Bob snorkeled for hours along the seawall.
On the edge of the ocean, he felt very small.
Yet after a while, Bob sensed it within.
His fear had subsided. His work could begin.

Bob was now ready to help the young seal

overcome all the worry and doubt she might feel.

Her diving was fine and her eyesight was great.

But she feared the deep water where older seals ate.

So day after day, they swam farther from shore,

building her confidence up more and more.

One morning, she dove down and swam out of sight,

and she fished on her own all that day and that night.

Bob was so proud that he quickly returned
to tell Miss Marine what young Kodi had learned.
But wouldn't you know that before he could do it,
Mama seal was so grateful that she'd beat him to it!

⇥ Chapter 2 ⇤

A Pelican's Plight

Then the next morning, Bob got a new task
when Mary Marine had a favor to ask.
"Please take this net to the end of the pier.
There's some garbage afloat there that we need to clear.
Xena can join you and help toss the net.
It won't take too long as a team, I would bet."

So on the edge of the pier, where the sea meets the sand,

they threw out the net, but it slipped from Bob's hand.

It sailed past its mark and continued to fly

'til it landed on Beck, who woke up with a cry:

"It seems you've confused me with all that debris!

Get rid of this net, please, and let me fly free!"

Now Bob turned to Xena, and she turned to Bob.

"I told you!" she said. "You have bungled this job!"

"You distracted me, Xena. You've got it all wrong."

Then Bob called to Beck, "We'll be back before long!"

As they ran down the beach, they encountered old Earl,
a clam who was expert at growing a pearl.
"Earl, please, you must help us! We have to free Beck!
He's stuck in our net and now Xena's a wreck.
She thinks it's my fault, but I think it's hers.
Can you help release him? The next step is yours."

"Slow down there, my friend! I would sure like to help.

But what I remember when caught in the kelp,

is to solve any problem, don't look to the past.

You have to stop blaming and take action fast.

Be willing to own any part you have played,

and see if apologies need to be made.

This challenge you face holds a lesson for living,

when you're responsible, fair, and forgiving."

"Oh, Earl, you're so right. And dear Xena, I'm sorry.
We each played a part in it—that's the whole story."
Then, thanking old Earl for his timely advice,
They went back to Beck, and they didn't think twice.

When they arrived, Beck was anxious but kind:

"Bob, will you please help me out of this bind?"

"Sure Beck, I can help. I just thought of a friend.

If she's around, then your plight's at an end."

So Bob searched the beach and he finally spied

Cathy the crab crawling out of the tide.

"Oh, Cathy!" called Bob. "Could you maybe assist

with this pelican friend in a bit of a twist?"

"Of course I will help," said the crab. "Do not fret."

And with clipper-like claws, she had soon snipped the net.

In half of the time that it took to get stuck,

Beck was set free and was touting his luck.

He said, "Come on, friends. There is work to be done!

These shallows need cleaning, and then we'll have fun!"

⇥ Chapter 3 ⇤
Safe Passage

With the shore squeaky clean and the fun underway,
Miss Mary Marine interrupted Bob's day.
"Now Bob," she said firmly, "please stop what you're doing
and help spread the word of a storm that is brewing.
Tell the dolphins and whales, and the porpoises too,
to find a safe place 'til this weather blows through.
On your way, visit Doc. He knows how dolphins speak.
But hurry along now, the forecast looks bleak."

Bob took this direction and picked up his oar,
and with Xena reluctant, set off from the shore.

Propped up on his rock, Doc was taking a snooze,
and Bob had to wake him to tell him the news.
When Bob touched Doc's flipper, it startled him so
that Doc's old black spectacles fell on Bob's toe.

Doc sat up at once, but his eyesight was blurry.
He squinted at Bob. "Who is there? What's the hurry?"
"It's Bob, sir, and Xena. A big storm is near!
We must warn all of the dolphins and whales around here."

"Don't worry my friends, you are in the right place.
I'll send you to Al and you won't have to race.
Al the dolphin sends sounds with a sonar technique
and communicates better than us when we speak.
Those whistles and clicks he sends out bounce right back,
so he knows where he is and is never off track.
And when he relays his vibrations to friends,
they'll all be alert to the warning he sends."

Bob patted Doc's shell, for old Doc was so wise,
and he rowed to see Al, who was caught by surprise.

Upon hearing the news, Al just thought for a bit.
"I will tell all my friends that a storm will soon hit.
But in order to make all the whales understand,
I'll have to ask Tom, the blue whale, for a hand."

Then Al dove below and he sent out some sounds;
whistles and clicks started making the rounds.
And with Tom's help, soon they all were aware.
It was time to lay low 'til the storm cleared the air.

Then something strange happened. Bob's boat picked up speed.

The dolphins were pulling with ropes of seaweed!

"You brought us a message we needed to hear.

Now, we'll bring you to shore anytime of the year!"

⋙ Chapter 4 ⋘
A Simple Reminder

Although the big storm only lasted three hours,
the following day was still cloudy with showers.
Bob's alarm didn't ring, so he missed his first class.
Then his mask to view fish had a crack in the glass.
So Bob was unhappy; a rare state of mind
for someone so generally cheerful and kind.

Then who should arrive, rolling up on the shore,
but Wallace, a walrus Bob met once before.
"Good day!" hollered Wallace. He flopped closer by.
"But why the sad face? Have your plans gone awry?"

"Hi Wallace. I'm sorry. I hate to complain.
But today is a day I could throw down the drain.
My mask is not working. I missed out on school.
I can't go out snorkeling or dive in the pool."

"Well, Bob," chuckled Wallace, "allow me this chance
to say a few words about your circumstance.
Things can and do happen, I humbly report,
that block steady progress or stop us just short
of a goal we have set, or a plan we have made,
or a target to hit, or a vision we've laid.
But the good news, my friend, is that you're in control
of a thing that can stop rotten luck on a roll.
Start counting your blessings, the big and the small.
You'll see that these roadblocks mean nothing at all."

"But Wallace," Bob asked, "How can I find a way
to turn things around on this terrible day?"

"I use a reminder; it's easy to do.
Just find a small stone that seems special to you.
Tuck it into your pocket or somewhere close by,
and touch it whenever the tide's low or high.
Think of the people, the creatures, the things
that make you feel grateful, or make your heart sing.
For when you give thanks for the blessings you've got,
you're expanding the good and improving your lot.
What's more, you'll find gratitude works in a way
to lighten your mood and to brighten your day."

This all seemed so simple! So Bob reached right down.
He chose a flat stone and he flipped it around.
He thought of the wonderful friends he had made,
the ocean he loved, and the fields where he played.
He truly was grateful for so many things,
including his job and the challenge it brings.

Then Bob skipped to his boat with a new attitude.

His outlook was bright and his faith was renewed.

⇢ Chapter 5 ↞
Diving Deep

A few short days later, Al came to see Bob.
He needed some help with another tough job.
"Dear Bob," Al reported. "A stingray is stuck.
Ray's tail snagged a fishing line down in the muck.
I tried to release him but can't set him free.
You need to dive down there immediately."

Bob paused for a moment, not sure what to say.
He only had scuba dived once, in the bay.

Then Xena spoke up: "Now Bob, listen to me.
Are you sure you are ready for diving the sea?
The deep is mysterious—dangerous, too.
If you go down alone, there's not much I can do."

Bob turned back to Al and said, "Xena is right.
I'm afraid to dive deep and be out of her sight."
"Well, Bob, you're in luck. I see Earl on the beach.
Earl will convince you that Ray's in your reach."
"We'll see," Bob replied, as he ran towards Earl.
His doubts were increasing; his mind was awhirl.

"Hi, Bob!" said the clam. "My, you look a bit down.
Can I help you to turn your expression around?"
"I hope so," said Bob. "But I'm really not sure.
See, a stingray is trapped, but my scuba is poor.
I'm starting to think that I'll never succeed
in my goal of assisting sea creatures in need."

"Now Bob, don't despair. You've done more than you know.

Success is a choice and a place you will go.

You chose to protect us. You can't go astray.

Your vision and goals are now leading the way.

Never give up on the dream you hold dear.

Keep doing your best and new paths will appear.

Remember persistence; it goes with success,

like a king with a queen in the great game of chess."

So Bob closed his eyes and he thought of his goal.

To scuba the deep was just part of his role.

He smiled and then, touching his gratitude rock,

saw himself saving Ray with assistance from Doc.

Bob collected his gear and yelled, "Let's get the Sage!"
and they woke the old turtle, still spry for his age.
"Of course, I will lead you, Bob. Just follow me!"
And soon Bob and Doc disappeared in the sea.

Doc led the way to the place Ray was stuck,

while Bob clutched the stone he had brought for good luck.

As Doc pressed the line that was holding poor Ray,

Bob used the stone's edge and he cut it away.

Ray was set free and so grateful for Bob,

who'd proved once again he was made for this job.

To learn more about
The Adventures of Blue Ocean Bob®
and view other titles in the series,
please visit www.BlueOceanBob.com.

About The Author

Inspired by his young son, Brooks Olbrys created *The Adventures of Blue Ocean Bob* storybook series to share timeless achievement principles with children. A graduate of Stanford University, the Fletcher School of Law and Diplomacy at Tufts, and the University of California at Berkeley Law School, Brooks is the founder of Children's Success Unlimited and a managing director at investment bank Ion Partners. He lives with his wife and son in New York City.

About The Illustrator

From a young age, Kevin Keele has enjoyed creating artwork in many forms: drawing, oil painting, digital painting, even stained glass. His work has been featured in numerous picture books, magazines, board games, and video games. Kevin is currently an artist for Disney Interactive Studios in Utah where he lives with his wife and two sons.